Sab Huang

Cloud Labour

黃麗群

搬雲記

Cloud Labour
Sabrina Huang

Translated by Lin King

First published in English by Strangers Press, Norwich, 2024
Part of UEA Publishing Project

Printed by
Swallowtail, Norwich

Series editors
Nathan Hamilton
Jeremy Tiang

Cover design and typesetting
Glen & Rebecca Robinson (www.glenandrebecca.com)

ISBN: 978-1-915812-67-4

ká-sióng was made possible through generous funding from the
Ministry of Culture, Taiwan; National Museum of Taiwan Literature;
and Literature from Taiwan.

CLOUD LABOUR

SABRINA HUANG

TRANSLATED BY LIN KING

黃麗群
SABRINA HUANG

1.

Cloud Work

THE KEY IS NOT TO BE MISLED by objects or ornaments that seem overtly symbolic, or to pay too much attention to things in prominent locations. A rusty crescent knife stuck inside a blue cake, for instance, would be best avoided. And if you come across a large sack hanging from the ceiling to the floor that looks like the stomach of a giant animal, definitely do not slice it open. Or a boxy cathode-ray tube television with slick fish gliding across its screen — leave it well alone. Or a three-faced rat. The more obviously symbolic a thing seems, the more likely it is to be wrong. Most often, clients can't describe what exactly they need you to move. Sometimes they can't even admit it to themselves in the first place. It's not a big deal if you touch those decorative things, but it's a waste of everybody's time if you do so, and time is always scarce. Such decorations are just fragmented marginal sensory information and as such can't be translated into coherent output.

5

搬雲記
CLOUD LABOUR

These were the foundational principles Sky could recall from Peacock's teachings.

Peacock said, 'It's important for a Proxy not to do too much, but also not too little. You don't have to think of this work as a big deal, but also don't think of it as *not* a big deal.' She added, 'Our job is to remove the thing we're looking for and ferry it to our own side. You could think of it as a kind of relocation service. In that sense, our work is a type of manual labour — except the baggage we move isn't physical.'

'Like a cloud transfer.'

'Well, clouds are technically physical, even if they're mostly made of air.'

'I meant like cloud storage. Like a data transfer.'

'Oh. Then — yes. Like that.'

Peacock rose to answer the door. It was a man who visited once a month, whom Sky had nicknamed Boring Man. There was nothing to see in Boring Man's facial features except facial features. Sky was curious what a person like that would need "moved," and while Peacock would never reveal the specifics, Sky could guess based on Peacock's condition in the days following. Sometimes she was enraged. Other times, she would cry for half the day.

Boring Man said, 'Hello, Sky.'

Sky let his head droop. 'Hello.'

'What did you have for lunch today?'

'A sandwich.'

'Was it good?'

Sky, still hanging his head, shrugged.

'Do you want to guess which hand the coin is in?'

Boring Man held up two fists. Sky's head stayed down.

'Alright,' Peacock said, 'Ma's got to work.' She hooked her pinkie finger in the back of Sky's collar and gave it a slight tug. 'You go upstairs and take a nap.' Then she and Boring Man walked through the mansion's many glass hallways towards the Inner Chamber.

黃麗群
SABRINA HUANG

It was already dusk, too late for a nap. Peacock's words simply meant there would be no dinner that day, for her work often lasted late into the night, after which she would always drink a lot of tea and eat a lot of butter cookies, then — without uttering a single word — sleep for a long, long time.

Sky lay on the living room sofa and traced with his eyes the grey, wavy patterns moulded into the ceiling. Peacock once told him that the colour was called 'Cosmos Grey'. After a while, he went into the kitchen and stood on tiptoe to reach for the cookie jar. He, like Peacock, ate a lot of butter cookies — crisp and sweet and large. Though he ate carefully, the cookies still collapsed into countless crumbs, which he caught with the front of his cotton shirt and later dumped into the pretty, translucent bin. Even in the span of those few minutes, the crumbs left a constellation of faint oily stains on the cloth. Being still a child, Sky did not have the vocabulary to fully articulate his feelings, but in the moment he intuited that, compared to the grey paint meant to evoke the mystical but unfeeling cosmos, the greasy stars on his shirt were more akin to a celestial mass grave.

The first person for whom Sky ever Proxied was his mother. This was by design. He was sixteen at the time, but he did not feel nervous, fearful, eager, or confused, because Peacock kept repeating she would not make the task difficult or complicated.

She said, 'My guess is it will be a very simple room. Maybe even simpler than all the Vat Brains you've practiced on before.'

'But Vat Brains are all dead,' Sky protested. 'They're easy — each one only has one thing inside. Living people are messy. How would I know what I need to move?'

'*I'm* not messy,' Peacock said. 'Don't worry, you'll know. You'll know as soon as you're in there. It's in your genes. When I logged in for the first time, I knew instinctively what I needed to move. Your grandpa told me he'd known too, and so did his father before him.'

She added: 'And, remember: don't pay attention to anything too obviously symbolic or poetic. Anything that looks like a metaphor is useless. It's just for show.'

'Then what do you want me to move?'

She smiled. 'It should be something very subtle.'

They made their way down the glass hallways. Outside, the flowering trees were in full splendour, as if the blossoms were fulfilling a promise made to nature. If Sky had been able to describe how he felt at the time, he would have called it a sense of fundamental ambivalence. He did not particularly want to log in to his own mother — very few adolescents would. He felt as though he was doing something malicious, even transgressive somehow. The placid expression on Peacock's face unnerved him.

Peacock and Sky were very wealthy; as the profession was hereditary, its income passed down from generation to generation, and the fees they could charge were substantial. Like other parents in the same line of work, Peacock had spared no expense in buying many Vat Brains on which Sky might practice. They had to be procured fresh, no later than seventy-two hours after the death of the donor. Following installation, Peacock would first log in herself. She wouldn't alter anything, but instead would make sure everything inside was clear and simple — nothing too overstimulating or age-inappropriate. She wouldn't allow Sky to operate on any that didn't meet the requisite criteria, perhaps one or two in every ten would make the grade. The steep cost of being so selective was no object. This might make the selection process sound mysterious or mystical. But really the only measure that mattered was whether the donor had met with a happy end or a quick, clean death. The issue was more that this was quite rare.

Sky was often bored to death during practice. He would lie in the Proxying cabin and inject himself with the drug that induced the liminal state between sleep and wakefulness required by the Proxying system in order to represent in his consciousness a sealed room. In ancient Tibetan Buddhist terms, this room would be the 'bardo'. In the bardo would be a door, which Sky would dreamingly walk through to complete the 'log in' process. The term 'log in' was a little misrepresentative, a bit of a misnomer, but language inevitably had its limitations. A more accurate explanation might be that the Proxying system would 'translate' the Vat Brain's most concentrated emotions into a new, virtual world. Yet even this description was to a degree untrue, for the room created by the Proxying system was not composed of actual memories — it was more a metaphor for memories. As the Proxy, his most important task was to remove the keyword from this metaphor, which in turn meant removing the most disturbing emotion in the host room and carrying it back to his own, closing the door, and 'logging off'. By the law of conservation, whatever he removed would retain its energy. The Proxying process accelerated the breakdown of said energy, but it was impossible to erase completely and so the retrieved artefact would need to be carried and, in a way, slowly digested — psychologically, emotionally — by the Proxy. Had these been living people rather than Vat Brains, they would then no longer suffer that particular negative emotion. The good thing was their memories otherwise remained untouched: there would not be any gaps in their life, no missing information, but the damage they'd suffered, in effect the trauma, would no longer exist. They would still be able to recall the events, but would feel nothing. This perhaps sounds callous but it was very practical. Once upon a time, people could only reach this state by letting time slowly bulldoze their feelings away, waiting out the psychological scratches and scabs. These days, however, people went through a breakup in the morning and stood tall by nightfall. In the near future, they may go through a breakup in the morning and be standing tall by the afternoon. There was no longer any need for ugly tricks or harsh words in divorce negotiations; everybody was very civil, very fair.

Alas, it was too late for the dead, so the donors could reap none of the benefits. Even so, though there was there was nothing of significance within these brains and Sky mostly performed the tasks perfunctorily, each practice round still left him exhausted — an exhaustion that felt largely pointless. Once, he opened the door and found himself in an empty classroom with a single old desk in one corner. He tried to pry the desk drawer open, but it was so firmly stuck that he ended up having to bring the whole thing back with him to the bardo. Then, for the next few days, his only sensation was hunger. Constant hunger. He wanted to eat wood, to eat pebbles even. He later conjectured that the Vat Brain may have come from a frail, old person who died at a moment of reminiscing about their boundless appetite back in their youth. Or perhaps the brain had belonged to someone who had died from choking on their food.

'If you do well enough, a customer will be able to sleep soundly at night next to somebody who beat them that same morning. All the bruises will look like love bites.'

'What? But that's awful.'

'We don't get to judge.' Peacock pushed open the door to the Inner Chamber. 'You don't need to and *shouldn't* ask the customer what happened. And even if they want to tell you, it's better to not listen. And whatever you do, never tell the customer what you removed. Don't let your words plant the condition back into their hearts.'

'But I want to ask *you* what you want me to remove.'

'We'll get to that later.'

Before entering the Proxying cabin, Peacock said softly: 'Incense.' Sky lit a handful of lilyturf grass and tossed it into the celadon incense burner filled with fragrant Floating Watermoss Spice powder. Peacock said: 'Clearance.' Sky then used a crystal pendant to gently strike a wide brass basin; its golden ringing resonated like a chorus of three dozen sacred beasts.

After she entered the Proxying cabin, Peacock whispered: 'Veil.' Sky picked up a long strip of silk the colour of a dark tongue and covered his eyes, forehead, and scalp. The silk was called Severance.

His mother's voice was soft through the cabin's speakers. 'Are you ready?'

'Yes.'

'Then let's begin.'

Sky inserted the index finger of his left hand into a wall opening about as deep as his first knuckle. The sensation was a little unsavoury, like picking someone else's nose, but Sky was too used to the feeling to pay heed. He found the sharp metal point at the bottom of the opening and pressed. After a millisecond of slight pain and numbness, he'd successfully logged in.

Sighing with slight dread, Sky opened the door. As expected, it opened into a sealed room, just like it always had in his many practice rounds. He tried his best not to think he was logging in to his mother. This was just an average little chapel. Or rather, a space that seemed like a chapel, but the stained-glass windows were haphazard quilts that showed no saints or biblical scenes, no crosses or statues with tortured faces. The ground was ankle-deep in still, cold sand, white at first glance but then not quite. Sky saw a large branch of cotton half-buried in the sand, and immediately understood what Peacock had meant by 'you'll know'. He picked up the branch, returned to the bardo, inserted the branch into the supple, flesh-like wall, and watched as it was slowly absorbed.

He was confused at first after logging out. 'It's weird. I feel fine — I feel safe.'

'That's right, you should be feeling pretty good.'

'Is that normal?'

'Of course not,' Peacock said. 'Under normal circumstances, no one would want you to Proxy away something like that.'

'What was it?'

'It was — well, you know how I'm always exhausted after I log off? That exhaustion is about fifty times what you feel after your practice sessions — maybe sixty. So I always eat a lot of butter cookies.

搬雲記
CLOUD LABOUR

What you removed just now was the feeling I get after eating butter cookies.' She brushed her tongue across her front teeth. 'Right now, there's no taste in my mouth at all when I think of those cookies.'

'Why did you want me to remove *that*?'

'Yes, ordinarily it would be a nice thing, wouldn't it?'

'Does it mean cookies won't taste any good to you in the future?'

'No, it doesn't work like that. The next time I eat them, I'll build up a little bit of that feeling again. A bit like calorie intake. What did you see?'

'I thought you said that I should never talk about it.'

'I'm teaching you. And I'm your mother. You can talk to me about anything.'

'There was a chapel with a lot of white sand. There was a cotton branch in the sand, so I took it away.'

'That's pretty good. Most people would probably only be able to see the sand — if they see anything at all.'

'But now I really want to sleep.'

'OK. Go sleep.'

For the next three days, Sky's sleep was as dark and gooey as melting asphalt, and all food tasted more flavourful and wonderful. Outside, the air grew dense with rain. In the garden, grass and fungus vied with each other for the sun.

In the old days, Peacock would sometimes say. *In the old days*, back in the era people used to call 'Modernisation', the word 'modern' was used as sort of a self-satisfied expression for casting off undesirable 'oldness' while carrying forward desirable 'traditions' and paving the way for a notional future. If they were the Modern era, did that mean other eras weren't modern? Peacock told Sky that people back then were very self-centred. But that wasn't the point. The point, she said, was generally to assert that 'Our lives would have been less pleasant in the old days.'

黃麗群
SABRINA HUANG

People back then used various terms. Sorcerer. Onmyoji, Yin Yang master. Inibs, ang'ipu, inep. Witch doctor. Necromancer. Shaman. Jishen. Spirit medium. Religious conman. Psychosis patient. Swindler psychic. Apparition. Possession. Exorcism. Spiritual cleansing. But things began to change after experiments on human subjects demonstrated that ninety-nine percent of people could not achieve a presence in the bardo. Countless subjects merely fell asleep. Researchers compared the backgrounds of the few who succeeded in Proxying, but no matter how they pounded their heads, they could not find any meaningful commonalities in the genetic makeups.

In the end, the story went something like this: two young individuals who first succeeded in the experiment — a man and a woman — fell in love. While exchanging the sweet nothings of courtship, chattering on about themselves and their families, they realised that they had both inherited certain supernatural abilities from their respective bloodlines. Things like being able to see the auras emanating from people's heads: red, green, blue, black, yellow, white, grey. Or, strolling down the street, hand-in-hand, they would be able to see something that was either a snake made out of mist or mist shaped like a snake; whatever the thing was, it would be slithering unnoticed between the legs of other pedestrians. Et cetera.

'The scientists eventually came to recognise that, however much they wished to replicate or control such abilities, or trigger them in others, this clearly hereditary trait was simply not visible on a chemical or physical level. Only certain people, people like us, could make this profession work, though our DNA seemed no different from those of others. And so now our social status is very different from what it used to be. We can earn money openly and legitimately, and the people in charge look after us because they believe they're the ones who need us most. You should be glad I gave birth to you in the right generation.'

Later in Peacock's life, she found herself bedridden for a whole year. Sky began to practice officially, and Peacock, for lack of anything else to do, began telling him more and more stories. 'Your biological father was a decent, talented man, though he was too weak for this line of work. We were good friends. As he carried the trait himself, I suggested he and I ought to have a baby, and that baby was you.'

This was information that Peacock seemed to regard as taboo when Sky was a child, but, in those final years, she relayed these things to him in a cheerful tone, as though reciting a children's poem.

Sky wasn't a fool. He always knew there had never been a coin in either fist. As a child, he hadn't liked to look directly at Boring Man, because he would sometimes see another face — an older man's face — transposed like tracing paper, narrowing Boring Man's eyes and pinching his nose. The older man's face wasn't scary. In fact, it was silly, and sort of irritating, such that it was almost comical. It would hiss: 'Grandfather. Grandfather.' And so Sky had deduced that Boring Man was very likely his biological father, but, by the time that Peacock began telling him all this, Boring Man's visits had long ceased. None of this had any effect on Sky. In the era of Proxies, so long as a person had enough money and a suitable Proxy, any suffering, tears, or hatred could drift away — like passing clouds. If you had the teeth punched out of your month, there was no need to swallow the blood and bear the loss — you only had to see a dentist. And Sky's own mother was the most agile of Proxies.

Peacock would sometimes ask Sky to log in to remove the feeling of flannel pyjamas, or a cat licking her heel, or receiving a pair of ivory earrings as a girl. Ivory, even though there had been no elephants in the world for many, many years now. Peacock told Sky that, in the old days, such feelings were referred to as 'the little things in life'.

Other times, Peacock would log in to Sky and Proxy away different kinds of 'negative energy', as it was known in now defunct terminology; or 'psychological non-performing assets' as was now the legal jargon used in Proxying contracts. Sky was sunlit every day. Not a cloud or care in sight.

Towards the end of Peacock's life, by which time she had spent nearly two years in bed, fragile as the white puff of a dandelion, the only thing that interested her was conversation. And the only conversations that interested her were about Sky's own perceptions of her.

'Don't think of me as cold-hearted, as too utilitarian,' she said.

'Don't worry.'

'I'm not selfish, you know. I raised you well, and society needs people like us, people who have the gift to do this work. People like us have a responsibility, and I've done the responsible thing by giving birth to and raising you. We enable the richest and most powerful people to be very mentally stable, and their mental stability means a safer world for everybody else.'

'You always made out like what we do is no big deal.'

'You were still young, I didn't want you to get too big-headed. Stop pacing, it's annoying.'

'Oh.'

Sky sat on the jade velvet bench at the foot of Peacock's bed and pressed his palm gently against the fabric, feeling the tension in the weave.

'You think too much about other people's business, Ma.'

'When people get old, they have nothing else to do. Sometimes I lie here and ruminate on things that have been interesting in my life, but it's all tasteless, like chewing on paper.'

Sky said nothing. After a moment, he asked, 'Ma, if it's uncomfortable, are you sure you don't want to be Proxied?'

'No. I've told you many times not to ask me that anymore. People like us — we spend our whole lives living inside other people's joys and sorrows. Now, any discomfort that I feel is my own. And that brings a kind of relief.'

Sky was silent again. His mother had been showing signs of mental disarray, her thoughts becoming scattered and untraceable. He realised he had never once asked her if she loved him. Perhaps he was the type of person who didn't need love, since people who had never suffered injury didn't yearn for relief. Or perhaps he was simply the type of person who didn't like to ask pointless questions.

One day, when Peacock was truly approaching her end, Sky went against his mother's wishes and wheeled her into the Inner Chamber on a gurney. He told her, 'Ma, focus on the feeling that's making you most uncomfortable. You can do it, Ma. Think of your greatest discomfort.' He added, 'I hope you can be at ease, Ma. I'd like you to go in peace.'

Watching his mother die, Sky had found his emotions growing more turbulent, rising and falling in great altitudes. He had never tried to work while he himself was so unstable, which he rarely was, but this was Peacock, the mother who had gifted him the sensations of eating butter cookies, of being licked by a kitten. He did not hesitate. Though it was risky, he was able to log in without a hitch. Once inside the bardo, he pushed open the door. Peacock's room was filled with people and things and non-people and non-things; every being that possessed a tongue was screaming; everything that had fingers was clawing and digging; the ground kept on undulating and swallowing. Sky did not have time to observe anything — he grabbed the Daruma doll he wanted and quickly exited.

He returned his dying mother to their home care aide and went to his bedroom to lie down. It was winter. The bedroom was large and the air was cold. It felt like time was crawling along the floor. Whatever substance had been used to paint the Daruma doll's dark eyes soon permeated Sky's body, seeping outward from within him. He tugged on his fluffy, snow-white blanket. The darkness was hatred — hatred of the healthy, hatred of those who could walk on two legs. This hatred was his mother's last kernel of dignity after three years in her sickbed. Sky could not tell whether this hatred included him. Reflexively, he wept for a long while. Afterward, he directed his AI assistant to call for a colleague who specialised in grief. An appointment was arranged for the following Monday. Emergency appointments such as this were a special privilege for fellow Proxies. Peacock's doctor had informed him his mother would not make it past Sunday.

2.
Stone

STONE HAD ALWAYS KNOWN she would one day meet Sky. There was nothing romantic or theatrical about this. Stone knew that she would meet Sky purely because she had received Sky's contact information from Distance — or rather, from Distance's eyes. They'd been lying in Distance's bed. Stone had said, 'You have a great bed, you know. A truly classical bed; patterned with a turtle's shell, four posts clawed with lion's feet, parquet panels shielding you from draft, sculpted from bishop wood inlaid with pomegranate wood — ka-tang lip tsióh-liú. A classic Red Sleeping Bed.'

'I had no idea,' Distance said. 'I only care that it's good for sleeping.' He half-rose to look at Stone. Face-to-face, eye-to-eye. 'I'm gonna introduce you to someone.'

'Who?' Stone asked. Stone used her right index finger to gently tap the outer corner of her left eye five times: one, two, three, four, five.

'Hey, I never noticed — you have a mole at the corner of your eye,' Distance said. Then: 'Alright, sent. This guy's name is Sky. If you want to sell, he'd probably buy. You told me to introduce you to a client, so — here you go.'

黃麗群
SABRINA HUANG

'The corner of one's eye used to be called the Adulterer's Gate, and supposedly governed relationships between husbands and wives. In the old days, nobody would've wanted to marry someone with a mole like mine.'

'You're so full of useless trivia,' Distance said. 'Adulterer's Gate. What an awful name.'

'You're always complaining. Why don't you just sleep with a robot?'

'Why don't *you* just sleep with a robot?'

'Robots don't have your vigour.'

'Uh-huh. Thanks.'

In reality, both Stone and Distance were exhausted. For Stone, it was a physical exhaustion from the mutually feral sex acts in which they'd been engaged just twenty minutes earlier. For Distance, the fatigue stemmed from Sky's visit a few days prior. People in their line of work tended to help each other out, Proxying for each other at half price and such. But the more Distance thought about it, the more he felt that he had the worst of the bargain; he did not have much use for Sky's specialty, and helping Sky had left him especially drained.

Distance's first impression of Sky was that he spoke very slowly. Sky had said, 'My mother left me your contact information, she is no longer with us.'

Distance immediately grasped the implications. 'I understand.'

Sky added, 'I guess I don't have to tell you what happened.'

'No, you don't.'

'My clients often want to tell me.'

'That's different,' Distance said. 'And I'm different from the others in our field. I specialise in grief, and grief is the only thing that's really private — everybody should reserve something for themselves. My guess is — and I apologise if I'm overstepping here — they probably just want to share things with you because you're young and good-looking. Do you hear them out?'

'Sometimes I want to, a little. But I never do.'

'In that case, I'm like you but also unlike you. Like you, I never listen — but in my case, I have no desire to. Let's begin.'

It took one glance for Distance to recognise Sky's blankness, his carefully nurtured tabula rasa. He was a classic case of how many people of their profession were raised: polished daily like a precious vase until they become literal — and very successful — vessels. Distance's upbringing had been a little different. In a sense, he was a true natural. As a very young child, his parents had asked him again and again why he did not cry after logging off a Vat Brain. He would ask in return: *Why would I cry?* His parents were confused, and only gradually came to the astonishing realisation that they had given birth to a child naturally immune to sadness. This was a tremendous gift, though a very cruel one — not to mention antisocial.

Unconsciously, Distance's parents began conceding to him on all matters. Over time, they stopped turning down his requests, and he was allowed to stay up past curfew and enjoy sweets as and when he pleased. Whenever he entered the living room, his parents' bodies would instinctively shift a little closer together, like a clam snapping shut. This made Distance deeply uncomfortable, which led him to forcibly shed a few appropriate tears after each practice. But everybody saw through the fakery — though nobody ever called him out — and it only made his parents even more fearful of him. The law strictly prohibited Proxies from removing fear, a crucial instinct for human survival. As such, his parents could not alter their feelings; they simply waited until he was of age, then politely relocated to another city. Since then, they met up only once a year, taking turns to host dinner: two meat dishes, one vegetable, one soup, one dessert, one overnight stay.

Distance now recalled he had yet to complete that year's annual pilgrimage. Just thinking about it made him drowsy. Stone's voice struck him like a gently tossed pebble: 'You know, we keep saying "sleep with," but we're never sleeping. There's no element of sleep in any of this. It's so trite how we can't help but use euphemisms.'

'Mm.'

'Did you actually fall asleep just now?'

'No. I just thought of something suddenly.'

'That guy you were talking about earlier — this Sky person. You really think he'll buy?'

'It's hard to say.'

'What's his specialty?'

'You can't tell by looking at him?' Distance suddenly brightened a little, perching his chin on top of Stone's shoulder, 'it's mainly hatred. More generally, it's pain. And *jealousy*. Hardcore stuff.'

'Jealousy? Shit.'

'That's why I started thinking you might be able to sell to him. He might be a good client for you. I used to do jealousy a long time ago, but I couldn't stand it, it was so unpleasant. It was so — I don't know — *rancid*. I'd have to take a long time after each appointment.'

'It's so easy for people like you to say such things — like oh, boo-hoo, I can't stand jealousy, jealousy's so nasty.'

'What do you mean, people like me? What people am I like?'

Stone took a second before replying. 'People who can't feel sadness. People who can't feel heartbreak or sorrow.'

'Bullshit. What you really mean is *people who have money*. People who from the moment they were born never once had to worry about how to make a living. People who help even richer people live more comfortably.'

'Your words, not mine.'

'So I should apologise to you and everybody else for being born into this?'

'You don't have to apologise, but you don't have to make jealousy sound so unseemly.'

'But I do find it unseemly. You can't choose what you're born into, but you can either choose self-discipline and self-betterment, or you can choose to be a bum, go with the flow, and rot with the trash that surrounds you.'

21

'Ugh, forget about it. I don't want to talk about this anymore. Self-betterment my ass. Anybody who can pay you people can afford to be pure and noble. It used to be that the filthy rich had to *pretend* to be pure and noble, but after you people came about, they can believe they really *are* immaculate. Their hearts are all unclouded, whereas people like me are wicked, putrid, beyond salvation.'

'If you're that jealous, ask *him* to Proxy you. Come back and sleep with me after he Proxies all that stuff away. No, not sleep. Come back and fuck.'

'Go to hell. As if I have the money for that.'

'You'll have money if you sell.' Distance was an extremely prudent man, and even in this context, he only used the ambiguous term *sell*. Stone usually appreciated his discretion, but in this case it left her displeased.

'Don't be stupid,' she said.

'Do you remember me telling you about someone named Auspice? She really disliked the idea of Proxies. She found it evil. And then her dog died, she wouldn't stop crying, so I was like, "If not me, then who?" and she was all, "Absolutely not." I thought about it and decided that she was right, it didn't seem appropriate, so instead I went and bought her a session for denial, anger, confusion, and despair. But she actually got mad at me! *Furious.* Screaming and yelling. She went and had the contract nullified, which really pissed *me* off. That package was really expensive, even with my discount, no refunds.'

'She definitely left you because of that.'

'That was much later.'

'No. That was *definitely* the reason.'

On her way home, Stone couldn't stop mulling over Distance's words. Was she jealous? Jealous of the beautiful women in Distance's life? It took eighteen flights of stairs for Stone to reach her apartment, a long enough trek to contemplate the gap between them. She thought of the adage, *A journey of any distance begins with a single step*. Distance's life probably felt like the beginning of countless journeys; Stone's life felt like being stepped on. She then thought of the adage, *One might send off a friend by walking a great distance with them, but in the end the two must part*. Distance's life was full of things that he would feel sorry to lose; Stone's life was only parting.

The building had one-hundred-and-one floors. It often loomed disproportionately large on old tourist maps, like a jade-coloured iron bar jabbed into the island's eye. It was gradually abandoned by the luxury boutiques and foreign businesses that it housed, and soon the masses began settling into the emptied rooms like ants. It began with the lower floors. At first they occupied the office spaces behind the storefronts, for the privacy afforded by the partitions which could each house one to two families. Then there were the storage rooms and the dressing rooms of erstwhile clothing stores, which were small but had lockable doors, thus acceptable for one occupant. The people who lived in the dressing rooms would stretch their legs through the gaps under the doors out into the hallways; so long as their faces were kept private, they didn't mind.

Rumour had it the building was considered state-of-the-art in its time, and once nicknamed the Millennium Building. Others claimed that this was false, that the Millennium Building was in an altogether different part of the city. Still others said that there was never any place of that name. In the early years, people took the dilapidated elevators. But after a few plummeted and others got stuck between floors, they all finally fell out of use. Some good Samaritans worked together to board up the doors for safety, but others complained they should have minded their own business — those unwilling to risk death could huff and puff their way up the stairs, and not deprive others of the small pleasure of playing Russian roulette.

Around this time, people were under the impression the world was on the verge of collapse, though people of all eras always thought things were falling apart. Human beings, in any millennium, believed they were clinging to the precipice of apocalypse.

When Stone first moved in, people had already filled almost twenty storeys, which was pushing the limit of endurance without the elevators. People had managed to build plywood partitions in the upper floors and even rerouted the plumbing and electricity, so the compartments were fairly organised and well-equipped. Each had a stove, a bed, and a toilet, plus a communal shower every six compartments.

Somebody with a sense of humour had installed a white marble statue of a urinating boy, but the carving was rough, the stone of poor quality, the urinary tract congested. In lieu of water, a cluster of silver wires had been wedged into the statue's hand. The residents would touch the wires when they passed until the dull strands gleamed; over time, they seemed to undulate and shimmer with more radiance than would a real stream. The wires originally pointed to the bare floor, but later some inspired person placed a tin gardening bucket underneath, even periodically adding water to it. This 'urine' may not have been convincing on its own, but the artistic touch made the intention amusingly clear. The tin bucket began to take on an almost noble significance. Was this not somehow emblematic of society? Stone kicked the tin bucket lightly when she passed. Everybody passing kicked it in either direction, and this back and forth somehow left the bucket more or less in the same place.

Stone had managed to secure an old refrigerator for her room. A fridge was an excellent thing; the motor hummed at a low frequency at the foot of her bed, providing a comforting background noise at night. Stone found this more comforting than the sound of human breathing, though the community was largely very safe — there was a neighbourhood watch every five floors, and, though most people kept one or two part-time jobs or worked night shifts to stay afloat, few people were so desperate they would behave recklessly towards a neighbour.

黃麗群
SABRINA HUANG

Stone opened the refrigerator, took out two hard-boiled eggs, opened a pack of dried seaweed, wrapped the peeled eggs in some of it, and took a bite. Protein, iodine, vitamin B. Then she leant against the metal desk by her bed and looked towards the window, propping her legs on the sill. Outside, the haze was unusually low and dense, pressing up against the glass like a chloroformed handkerchief being held to an abductee's face. The egg and seaweed tasted strange together, but not in a bad way.

Stone did not usually spend her time thinking about Distance. Was she really jealous of him? Or, to be more precise, envious? She licked at the grains of salt around her lips. It didn't really matter either way. Perhaps without at least a little jealousy, a little malicious intent and frisson, they would not have suited each other so well in bed — they would not feel so evenly matched. Perhaps a little resentment gave rise to the most vivid of feelings.

Stone felt like she needed something else to eat. Something hot. She decided to order takeout and, as she waited for a drone to ferry chicken ramen up eighteen floors, she projected the information about Sky from her iris transmitters. She saw something ineffable in the holographic image of his face, as though she was looking at the interior of a vessel: like a reality that existed, but not fully in anyone's consciousness. She was intrigued. Yes — in the not-so-distant future, she would pick an auspicious day to pay a visit.

3.
Dewdrop

THE CERAMIC TILES WERE TOO WHITE. So white it seemed the very concept of black, or the concept of colour itself, had been outlawed. 'White' came in many varieties: silk, moonlight, snow, ermine, powder (grainy), tofu (fragile), ivory and jade (hard and gleaming), water and cloud (soft and shifting). But the whiteness of these tiles was like the apogee of all whites: so unequivocally pure all other forms of white seemed 'dirty'. This made no sense, for while one could have dirty blue or red or brown, 'dirty white' was merely a type of grey. The flawlessness of this whiteness was therefore no longer even symbolic or metaphorical; it was a matter of irrefutable technical difference.

黃麗群
SABRINA HUANG

The room was the size of two parking spaces, completely covered in white tile, even the ceiling. As soon as he entered, Sky was at a loss. Though this was a subconscious space, one in which his feet and hands did not really exist, he nevertheless felt as though he had no place within such clarity. What on earth was he supposed to remove? There was not a single object here. He began to feel a slight panic, he had less than two hours. Beyond this, as many unfortunate experiments had previously revealed, there was an increasing risk that the subject would develop an irrational yet extremely powerful sense of connection with the Proxy. That was the clinical description; to the subjects, what they felt was 'love'. This could even prove fatal: one subject grew so obsessive they eventually murdered their Proxy, others had killed themselves.

So in order to protect both parties, the system forcibly logged out the Proxy after eighty minutes and recorded the session as a failure, which guaranteed a full refund. But it was not the financial loss that Sky feared, rather the sudden revelation of the limitations of his own talent; that it was manifestly insufficient for the task at hand. He felt as though he had been tricked; led into a spotless bathroom, believing he would discover something inside, only to then find himself locked in and abandoned. A bit shaken, he told himself again and again: *don't rush, don't rush, there's no need to rush.*

The tiles remained tiles. No patterns, no cracks, no geckos, spiders, webs; not even a speck of dust.

Sky hadn't expected such a dilemma from his first encounter with Dewdrop. She'd entered first, her father following behind. The intake form showed that Dewdrop had just turned fourteen. While this was the age at which most humans were at their physical ugliest or most malformed, Dewdrop's features seemed made of glass. Her silhouette was shaped like fine china, her hair was like threaded gold.

搬雲記
CLOUD LABOUR

She was sharp and coquettish. Her clothing was full of embroidery, tassels; she wore a lightweight leather armour with petite bells and precious metals adorning her collar, wrists, hairline. She was like the walking embodiment of some kind of ceremony.

Sky had served many young clients before. All were beautiful, formed from sperm and eggs meticulously selected for the best possible genes. But Sky had never let his guard down, for these young people were frequently very complex. Their complexity originated from a certain purity of heart; by comparison, the supposed complexity in adults was in fact easier to deconstruct. Any darkness of purpose or aim would have a simple fix — those who felt aggrieved needed their grievances removed, those who felt entangled needed their knots untied. As such, they were simple. But the minimalism of these youths' suffering made things all the more dangerous because it was so lacking in apparent motive. But such a blankness, imbued almost with a childish playfulness, lack of direction, could build up to a truly unassailable and indefatigable evil.

So, Sky did not like to work with such younger clients. He recalled a girl by the name of Mica, not much older than Dewdrop, who had seemed pitiable in every way, whose sorrow seemed boundless, who could not get out the words, whose wordlessness only made the sentiments stickier. When Sky logged in, he'd seen a palatial room made of gold and bright gems, of intricately sculpted beams and columns, of gilding and vermeil, of fine and invaluable crystal mirrors reflecting each other infinitely, of countless pots and plates stretching on and on. He had removed a single teacup from a cabinet in the centre of the room. It had a family insignia and chip in its golden rim.

'This is just wonderful,' Mica had said gently when she emerged from the Proxying cabin. 'It feels so great to be able to forgive them.'

Sky, who'd been tired, hadn't responded. Mica, with even more exquisite gentleness, had pressed on: 'I'm not valued by anyone around me. They just see me as a normal, pretty girl. That's something I've always had to endure. I've accommodated it and worked hard to try to prove myself, to earn their heartfelt recognition, to make them see I'm not on the same plane as everybody else. You have to understand — if we were to deconstruct a person down to their pedigree, appearance, talents, knowledge, temperament, interests, the depth of their interiority, there's not a single aspect of me that's lacking in any way. How difficult is *that*? *Too* difficult. People shouldn't be treating me as if I'm on the same plane as others. That's *unfair* to someone like me. But, miraculously, I've completely forgiven them! I don't expect you to understand the feeling of —' Sky had cut her off brusquely. 'Of course I understand. Stop talking. I don't need to and don't want to and shouldn't have to know the details of your personal life. That goes against the foundational principles.'

He had started to digest Mica's pain, and was already feeling a little out of control. Her pain had been a poisonous resentment — the fastest-acting kind, with the longest-lasting recoil. The heft of a person's felt pain was not necessarily proportionate to the inducing incident. In Mica's case, while the incidents had been petty, the pain was enormous, akin to that of a virtuosic pianist who had lost both arms in a car accident.

Sky could offer no commentary on this. He tried his best to maintain his professional ethics, reminding himself that pain was subjective and could not be evaluated by others. All pain had equal value, or at least his fee was always of equal value, and he had no reason to appraise in relation.

Mica had looked at him with pity in her eyes. 'You really don't understand at all. Even now, I can forgive you completely. Forgiveness is a noble and special feeling — it's not something everybody can understand.'

Sky did not know if Dewdrop would also be this way. Dewdrop's father, a large-bellied man with a voice like a gong, said a little sulkily that this was the only thing Dewdrop had wanted for an early fifteenth birthday present. 'Nobody in our family does this. We keep asking her why she's unhappy, but she won't say.' Dewdrop only smiled.

Dewdrop's father owned every commuter ferry and about half the tourist boats between the basin city's many lakes and small islands; in addition, he also dabbled clandestinely in operations selling weapons, clean water, and medication. Dewdrop, meanwhile, owned her father. The pair were trailed by eight bespoke, humanoid bodyguards, each exactly 190 centimetres tall with golden bodies and red faces — an ostentatious display. Dewdrop's father boasted happily, 'My daughter named them all — I can never remember. Tell him.'

Dewdrop nodded. 'They're Blue Bastion, Yellow Yielding, Red Roar, White Water, Safety, Remedy, Sagacity, and Great Spirit.'

Sky thought these were silly names. 'Which is which?' He asked, thinking they all looked identical.

'Whichever,' Dewdrop said.

This amused him. 'Isn't the whole point to distinguish between them?'

'It's more a feeling,' Dewdrop's father said. 'They don't answer, no matter what you call them anyway.'

Sky left Dewdrop's father in the waiting room, which had a curved wall and a holographic projector, where he ordered beef noodles and Tieguanyin tea, then added cha siu bao after a moment's consideration. There were also sleeping pills if he felt tired, as well as a new piece of hardware that Sky had just installed a few days prior: if guests decided they did not wish to do anything except to sit quietly, they only had to press a button and the colour would drain from the flooring within five seconds, revealing with perfect clarity the rippling wild reeds of the mountain underfoot. Dewdrop's father, seeming contented, said, 'Take your time. Hey, Blue something, Yellow, Red, White whatever — go with Dewdrop. The other four stay here.' The bodyguards did as instructed.

'Huh — so they *do* seem to know their own names,' Sky observed.

'Nah, they don't,' Dewdrop said. 'They just understood the order was for four to stay and the other four to come with us.'

'Fascinating.'

Sky led Dewdrop out of the room.

The two of them said nothing as they walked, because there was nothing to say. Sky saw no point in making small-talk when he was about to receive something Dewdrop could not articulate anyway. With this imminent, chit-chat seemed insincere, and irritating.

Dewdrop, meanwhile, was thinking very highly of Sky. She thought him most deserving to be included in her future. He seemed to her a little vacant, his reactions a little slow — any slower and he'd have been obtuse, but this was just the right amount of lag. Of course, everybody in his profession seemed a little vacant and obtuse. The best thing about Sky was that he was mostly alone — and young. Not that somebody older wouldn't have worked, they just wouldn't have been as good.

When they reached the Water Hall, Dewdrop asked, 'Do you not chat with your clients?'

'Not really.'

'I've never done this before — I'm so excited.'

'Mm. Are you nervous?'

'Is there something I need to be nervous about?'

'No. Some people don't like how the room looks, but you won't be able to see anything once you enter the cabin anyway, so it's nothing to worry about. Do you need some water? Restroom?'

'Nope, I'm good.'

Dewdrop did not dislike the look of the Inner Chamber at all. She thought it beautiful, with its brimming red light, paper lanterns, central shrine furnished with all kinds of small objects that Dewdrop could not name — many of which, in fact, even Sky could not name, but which had been passed down to him from generations past. Every object allegedly once had a use and significance but by now all were largely decorative. The steely Proxying cabins were welded into one of the walls, and the three remaining walls were thick and covered densely with wooden figurines: buffalo and horses, giant turtles, boa constrictors, guardian lions, pitch-black tigers, gargoyles, chimeras, and Ganesha the elephant-headed god.

'Woah. Can I touch them?'

'Sure.' Sky began lighting the incense, ringing the brass plate, and covering his face with red silk. Dewdrop did not watch, but instead stroked and studied the different sculptures, apparently enjoying herself.

'Ready?' Sky asked.

'Yup.'

Sky was at a loss. He began slapping the tiled walls, searching for some kind of defect. Was there perhaps a hidden door? But a hidden door would have been dreadful, too. There was a saying in their profession: *Door within door, disaster or death*. An inner door meant that the client's condition was extremely poor, that their inner demons were too deeply entrenched and had taken root, that they were already gnawing away at the life source. In such cases, the Proxy would generally choose not to open the inner door but to log off immediately. Even that would have been a better situation than the one in which Sky found himself. An inner door would at least have offered a valid excuse for exiting and some kind of resolution. Sky stepped on the tiles one by one, stomping down hard to see if any would show signs of loosening. None did.

He sat down in the centre of the room, hugging his knees. He rose, then sat down again. He entertained the possibility that this was a prank or a test. He'd read about such things in classic novels, legends of people who battled each other with their powers: one practitioner would animate a whole army of paper cut-outs; their opponent would wave a flag at the sun and transform it into a gourd that sucked up the paper army; the paper-user would laugh coldly and ring a little copper bell hidden in his sleeve, making the gourd swell until it eventually exploded into a useless lambskin pouch... Sky, returning to himself from these meandering thoughts, saw that his non-existent white trousers had been dyed red. Alarmed, he leapt to his non-existent feet only to see that his shirt and trousers were as clean as ever. In the interval, blood had seeped up from the cracks of the tiled floor.

'I see.' He let out a breath. 'These kids are too much.'

The liquid *looked* like it *ought* to be blood, but he could not confirm this. There was neither a lot nor a little. It was in the shape of a hand, and had an eerie surface tension that seemed to be distending.

The question was how he would remove it. He instinctively wiped at it. Left hand, right hand, both hands. His palms remained deathly white. He rubbed and rubbed, but the blood maintained both shape and texture without a trace of disturbance. Sky's hands felt neither cold nor warm. His nose detected no rankness, no metallic scent. Nothing about the blood had any real connection with life. Sky fell to his knees, again at his wit's end.

After staring into space for a while, something finally occurred to him. He got down on his stomach, stretched out his legs and arms, lowered his face, and began to lick. The handprint slowly halved. Three fingerprints, the thumb, the single pinkie, the smallest knuckle, the fingertip. Sky got up. There was a total absence of taste in his mouth, but he felt a certainty the liquid had indeed been blood.

It had been the first time since becoming a Proxy that he had been so panicked, so stumped, so completely unsure of whether he had succeeded. What sort of weight awaited him after Dewdrop left this chamber, her own burden lightened?

He opened the cabin door and staggered outside, panting as though he had sprinted across the whole of the world. Propping himself against the wall, he stared at Dewdrop's silent face in the neighbouring cabin, still inert. Back in the waiting room, Dewdrop's father had long finished his beef noodles and cha siu bao, and had ordered himself some red bean soup for dessert. He was, in that moment, admiring the colours of the evening sky — the gelatinous consistency it took on right before plunging to full darkness. Outside the Inner Chamber's door stood the four humanoid bodyguards, looming motionless.

4.

Open Door

IT WAS A HEARTLESSLY CLOUDLESS DAY. Fierce sunlight burst into every space, so extravagantly beautiful it seemed to mock anybody who could shed a tear on such a day. When Sky opened the door, the first thing he did was to prise Peacock's professional nameplate off its front. 'Peacock' embossed with blue-green cloisonné enamel. Sky's own name was carved into a slab of black slate. He placed her nameplate with the clothing and other belongings he had sorted through.

All these things felt easier after his appointment with Distance; no psychological strain whatsoever. The only reason he'd procrastinated was because the Daruma doll had been so difficult to digest. On a rational level, Sky knew the hatred he'd taken in hadn't been his own, but still there were several times he found himself glaring hatefully at his own two legs for hours. This was a professional injury of sorts. Sky could not fully differentiate between whether this hatred belonged purely to Peacock or also came from a part of himself. Seawater had coursed up the rivers until big and small lakes formed all over the basin-shaped city. People relocated deeper into the island's centre and higher up its mountains as decent living spaces had become increasingly scarce. He, meanwhile, lived in a grand mansion above the clouds, the suites connected by glass corridors and rooftop gardens. Could it be that he hated this life?

He regretted slightly that he hadn't obeyed Peacock's wishes. Why had he chosen to Proxy her against her will? Out of kindness? Love? Maybe so, but he knew that he had also done it because he didn't want to risk being haunted by her regrets. He began to understand why Peacock had isolated him on this faraway mountain ever since he was a child, for otherwise he may very well have imploded by now. At the same time, he was aware that this distance from the rest of society prevented gaining a degree of understanding of the world and its meaning, or lack thereof.

Sky managed generally not to dwell on such things by working with clients every day. He now stood in front of the mirrored wall and told himself: *This is a meaningful thing to do. There is nothing more meaningful in the world than bearing another's pain.* Albeit for a fee.

He had one appointment that day, someone by the name of Stone.

She arrived looking courteous and wearing a well-made white shirt that extended past her knees to her shins; like a cold mist pouring down a mountain from its peak. Her shoes were inky green. Sky intuited that something was off; he saw at a glance that Stone could not possibly be a real client of his, then had a strange sensation that he should give Stone some of the clothes Peacock had left behind.

In this era, the true marker of wealth was a certain facial expression — not of serenity, per se, but sterility.

Stone's face, he could tell, had been smoothed out, but through her own effort. It still showed traces of all kinds of human emotion — not physical signs of wear and tear, more like a dazzling display of everyday life: like a dinner table, a garden. Most of his clients had been getting Proxied since the legal age of fourteen, but one look at Stone's face was enough to tell him this was not the case for her. Sky hesitated; referrals from fellow Proxies were usually reliable, but he still preferred clients who came from money. This was not just prejudice but a practical concern, because the condition of being wealthy was not about gain — *I have this, I bought that* — but lack, as in 'I don't have any experiences with the feeling of deprivation.' Clients who started from deprivation and progressed to wealth, however, tended to be much more complicated.

'I'm Stone.'

'I know.'

'Your place is really hard to find.'

'True. It's not easy.'

'But it's very beautiful.' Stone looked about. The parlour was surrounded by silver-framed glass windows that made the space resemble a crystal box, suggesting the people sitting within it to be jewels. A vivid landscape filled the windows, the clusters of the variously sized lakes visible into the distance. 'I didn't know that places like this existed.'

'This was called Catspace on the old maps. But it's rare for the weather to be this good. It rains a lot around here, and even when it's not raining, there's usually a lot of fog.'

'That's such a funny name,' Stone said, smiling. 'I'll bet it rains cats and dogs. Was the mountain across from it called Dogspace?'

Sky shrugged. 'It's possible.'

'I'll be honest — Distance gave me a referral, but I didn't come here for a Proxy.'

Sky nodded. 'I felt that that might be the case. So... how may I help you?'

'I have a business proposal.' Stone's expression altered very slightly, but the change was enough to make her seem a different person entirely, a dinner table losing its candle, a garden its bees or flowers.

'A business proposal?'

'That's right.' Stone nodded.

Pleasure Vendors secretly sought out Proxies as buyers, but what they sold was their opposite: all sorts of good moods, whether high-spirited or mellow — harmony and happiness. This was highly illegal. Not only were Pleasure Vendors frowned upon for exchanging feelings like parental love or childhood memories for money, there were vendors who, in order to secure a large supply of 'goods', purposely sought out extreme and depraved forms of pleasure to sell.

Many viewed Pleasure Vendors as almost antihuman, and transactions with them were inevitably regarded as serious ethical violations and a threat to society at large. In the most severe cases, a guilty Proxy could have their license revoked, and the Vendor almost always served a long prison sentence. Sky thought Stone very bold.

'Aren't you afraid?' he asked.

'Of what?'

'Aren't you afraid I'll report you?'

'For what?' Stone looked bewildered. 'Maybe I'm a plainclothes investigator trying to set you up.'

'I don't feel that you are.'

She laughed. 'Maybe I'm not. But anyway, I don't think you would report me.'

Sky smiled back, though he knew he ought to put an end to this conversation and politely ask Stone to leave. But seeing as this appointment slot had already gone to waste, he figured it may as well serve as a mental break. He hadn't done much chatting with anybody since Peacock passed away.

'OK, let's assume that you *are* a plain-clothed investigator. I'd like to ask you something I assume you would be very knowledgeable about.'

'Please.'

'How do Pleasure Vendors guarantee Proxies get what they want? What I mean is, isn't there a risk that the Proxy might complete the moving process only to realise what they took from the Vendor wasn't what they wanted? Wouldn't that risk great loss?'

Stone cleared her throat, straightened her collar and spine, and adopted a bureaucratic demeanour. 'Sir. That doesn't usually happen. Some Vendors have been known to sign a contract with the Proxy, either by hand or biometric authentication. Both parties then deposit an amount equal to the Proxy's one-time service fee into a third-party account. If there are any issues after the Proxying transaction, the full deposit will be transferred to the Vendor's account. If the Vendor somehow cheats the Proxy with the wrong goods, the full deposit will be transferred to the Proxy's account. This minimises losses. The contract itself serves as leverage for both parties and is immediately destroyed after the transaction is complete. Of course, there are people who choose to forgo this and rely instead on an intermediary whom both parties trust.'

'That sounds complicated — and still risky.'

'Of course there are risks — it's an illegal transaction.' Stone said, chuckling. 'But, rationally, it's not worth the risk for a Vendor to cheat a Proxy, knowing that they will go to prison if exposed, whereas a Proxy would merely lose their license. On the other hand, a Proxy cheating a Vendor could lose their license, and therefore their livelihood.'

'If everybody behaved so rationally, my profession wouldn't exist.'

At this, Stone cocked her head and was silent for a while. Then she smiled and said, 'Then maybe I'm naive.'

'For you — uh, I mean, what's the most common type of transaction that you've witnessed?'

'An intermediary. People don't want to risk leaving evidence around. A trustworthy intermediary is still more reliable than a machine, because a machine might fall into the hands of someone untrustworthy. *But* if a machine is human-like, then it's also unreliable.'

'That's true,' Sky said. 'Machine-like humans are more trustworthy than human-like machines.'

'Overall, the probability of human kindness is low.'

'According to my mother, it's because people back in the day were too narcissistic.'

Stone nodded enthusiastically. 'Makes a lot of sense.'

'In any case, I've certainly learned a lot from this conversation. But —'

Stone cut him off. 'Have you ever considered *really* broadening your horizons?'

'… No.'

'Why not? Do you not feel the need? Or are you afraid?'

'No. Because you're a plainclothes investigator, so "no" is the only possible answer I can give.'

Sky hadn't meant to be funny, but these words somehow made him sound wry. A stranger in a well-made white shirt had exerted a certain force on the other party, bringing out traces they had never seen in themselves. Most interpersonal relationships had to do with people wishing to see themselves in others, in ways that suited or betrayed their own expectations, or, dysfunctionally, their loathings. That was why people needed others to exist, looking outward to peer more deeply and infatuatedly into themselves. This was a lonely thought. Sky began to feel a little anxious.

'Well, since I'm investigating, might I at least tour your workspace?' Stone did not move; she was still leaning back comfortably in the armchair, but it felt as though she was drawing nearer and nearer. Sky said nothing. He found himself rising to his feet.

They walked out of the reception room and through the Water Hall in the centre of the house. It contained a shallow pool, motionless and crystalline, surrounded by nameless plants and mossy rocks. The bottom of the pool was laid with large tiles of black slate and on the surface were narrow pathways, also made of black slate, just wide enough for one person to cross at a time.

The pathways radiated outward from a small circular island, each leading to a different wing of the large house. On the central island stood a tall table, which bore a clay pot of bonsai pine mounted on a pearwood rack. Sunlight showered down from the skylight.

'Water is very useful to us,' Sky said. 'The water here is called Yin Yang Water. It's half room-temperature well water and half rainwater that's been filtered and distilled.'

Stone, walking behind him, showed no emotion. She put on an ignorant yet interested voice to ask, 'What do you mean by useful?'

'Hm. How can I explain... for absorption? Filtering? In any case, water is useful for lightening some of the load before and after we work.'

'I see. I thought you were going to say it was the fruit of your labour — that the water symbolises a million different types of human tears, or something.'

'No, that's not my specialty. Or maybe I should say my clients don't usually come to me for those kinds of concerns.' Here, Sky thought suddenly of Distance. From appearances alone, Distance seemed like an undependable middle-aged guy, what with his dark crewneck sweater and colourful, clashing shirt collar poking out at the neck. But somehow people who put their undependability on display tended to be the more dependable. Distance lived in the city, with an office full of clutter. When Sky visited, he had to wait as Distance moved aside all sorts of knickknacks so they could pass through: a crimson Tengu mask, a rusty iron cowbell, triangular flags with bright yellow tassels, a small drum, and a big-bellied glass jar filled with what looked like seeds. Yet the mess was just like the creator of the mess, and both forced Sky to use a double negative: 'not unlikable'.

Sky thought about how Distance was likely a client of Stone's. He considered the stranger behind him and thought about how something that was once the best thing to have happened in this person's life, something unattainable except by chance, had perhaps already been consumed. Gone forever.

Sky grew aware of a certain emotion — one with which he was only too familiar. He turned back and asked, 'You said you learned about me from Distance. Which means Distance also had —' he paused for a second, searching for a pliable word, '— interactions with you.'

Stone shook her head. 'No.' Then: 'We're friends. Friends don't do business.' Stone sounded suddenly fatigued, but also as though she had more to say. She sighed lightly, then tapped Sky's shoulder with a finger. 'It's okay, I won't "inspect" you today. I'm sorry to have taken up so much of your time.' She knew that, if she wished to do business with this person, now was the best time to take her leave.

As Sky was seeing Stone out, he noticed someone down the far end of the slope. The person was looking in their direction without making much effort to conceal their prying gaze. Stone seemed to have noticed too, but she said nothing, and so Sky also said nothing. Both were thinking the same thing: *There really is a plainclothes inspector? No way*. Both had only ever heard rumours of such figures. They grew immediately suspicious.

Suddenly, Stone spun around, wrapped her arms around Sky's neck, and put on a show of being grieved by their parting. She kept rubbing her eyes as though on the verge of tears, but in fact turned off the transmitters in her irises. She said, with her lips under the lobe of Sky's ear: 'I have some truly excellent stuff — five-year-old-kid-eating-ice-cream-for-the-first-time type of excellent. Definitely worth it. Without a doubt.'

Then, feigning an outburst of heartache, she shoved him away and stalked off in the opposite direction of the watcher, who seemed to lose interest and slowly plodded away. All that remained was Sky, alone with his racing heartbeat, his quickened breaths.

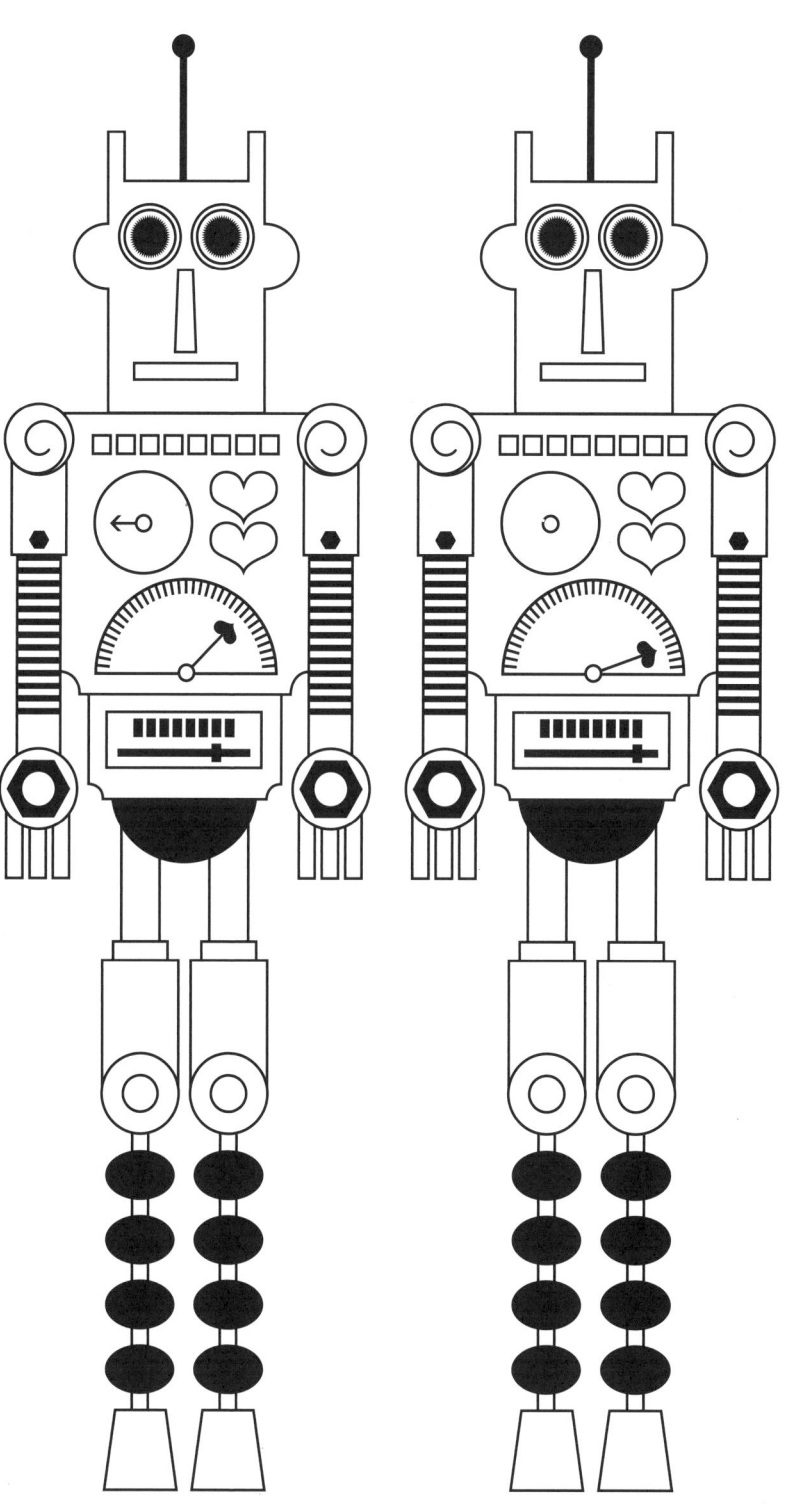

ká-sióng, from the Taiwanese romanisation of 假想, which means make-believe, imagine, hypothesise — derived from 假/ká meaning 'false' and 想 'sióng' meaning 'thinking', so 'false thinking' / imagination / hypothesis — is the latest series of new translations from Strangers Press, the people who brought you Keshiki and Yeoyu.

This time out we are featuring writers and translators from **Taiwan** in a set of five thrillingly distinctive chapbooks expertly curated in partnership with series editor, Jeremy Tiang, and exquisitely designed with our customary flair. The perfect pick-me-up for the literary curious, each carefully selected story is full of piercing insight and intrigue.

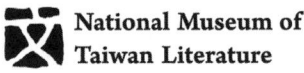